THE BOXCAR CHILDREN
SURPRISE ISLAND
THE YELLOW HOUSE MYSTERY
MYSTERY RANCH
MIKE'S MYSTERY
BLUE BAY MYSTERY
THE WOODSHED MYSTERY
THE LIGHTHOUSE MYSTERY
MOUNTAIN TOP MYSTERY
SCHOOLHOUSE MYSTERY
CABOOSE MYSTERY
HOUSEBOAT MYSTERY
SNOWBOUND MYSTERY
TREE HOUSE MYSTERY
BICYCLE MYSTERY
MYSTERY IN THE SAND
MYSTERY BEHIND THE WALL
BUS STATION MYSTERY
BENNY UNCOVERS A MYSTERY
THE HAUNTED CABIN MYSTERY
THE DESERTED LIBRARY MYSTERY
THE ANIMAL SHELTER MYSTERY
THE OLD MOTEL MYSTERY
THE MYSTERY OF THE HIDDEN
    PAINTING
THE AMUSEMENT PARK MYSTERY
THE MYSTERY OF THE MIXED-UP ZOO
THE CAMP-OUT MYSTERY
THE MYSTERY GIRL
THE MYSTERY CRUISE
THE DISAPPEARING FRIEND MYSTERY
THE MYSTERY OF THE SINGING GHOST
MYSTERY IN THE SNOW
THE PIZZA MYSTERY
THE MYSTERY HORSE
THE MYSTERY AT THE DOG SHOW
THE CASTLE MYSTERY
THE MYSTERY OF THE LOST VILLAGE
THE MYSTERY ON THE ICE
THE MYSTERY OF THE PURPLE POOL
THE GHOST SHIP MYSTERY

THE MYSTERY IN WASHINGTON, DC
THE CANOE TRIP MYSTERY
THE MYSTERY OF THE HIDDEN BEACH
THE MYSTERY OF THE MISSING CAT
THE MYSTERY AT SNOWFLAKE INN
THE MYSTERY ON STAGE
THE DINOSAUR MYSTERY
THE MYSTERY OF THE STOLEN MUSIC
THE MYSTERY AT THE BALL PARK
THE CHOCOLATE SUNDAE MYSTERY
THE MYSTERY OF THE HOT
    AIR BALLOON
THE MYSTERY BOOKSTORE
THE PILGRIM VILLAGE MYSTERY
THE MYSTERY OF THE STOLEN
    BOXCAR
THE MYSTERY IN THE CAVE
THE MYSTERY ON THE TRAIN
THE MYSTERY AT THE FAIR
THE MYSTERY OF THE LOST MINE
THE GUIDE DOG MYSTERY
THE HURRICANE MYSTERY
THE PET SHOP MYSTERY
THE MYSTERY OF THE SECRET MESSAGE
THE FIREHOUSE MYSTERY
THE MYSTERY IN SAN FRANCISCO
THE NIAGARA FALLS MYSTERY
THE MYSTERY AT THE ALAMO
THE OUTER SPACE MYSTERY
THE SOCCER MYSTERY
THE MYSTERY IN THE OLD ATTIC
THE GROWLING BEAR MYSTERY
THE MYSTERY OF THE LAKE MONSTER
THE MYSTERY AT PEACOCK HALL
THE WINDY CITY MYSTERY
THE BLACK PEARL MYSTERY
THE CEREAL BOX MYSTERY
THE PANTHER MYSTERY
THE MYSTERY OF THE QUEEN'S JEWELS
THE STOLEN SWORD MYSTERY
THE BASKETBALL MYSTERY

The Movie Star Mystery
The Mystery of the Pirate's Map
The Ghost Town Mystery
The Mystery of the Black Raven
The Mystery in the Mall
The Mystery in New York
The Gymnastics Mystery
The Poison Frog Mystery
The Mystery of the Empty Safe
The Home Run Mystery
The Great Bicycle Race Mystery
The Mystery of the Wild Ponies
The Mystery in the Computer Game
The Mystery at the Crooked House
The Hockey Mystery
The Mystery of the Midnight Dog
The Mystery of the Screech Owl
The Summer Camp Mystery
The Copycat Mystery
The Haunted Clock Tower Mystery
The Mystery of the Tiger's Eye
The Disappearing Staircase Mystery
The Mystery on Blizzard Mountain
The Mystery of the Spider's Clue
The Candy Factory Mystery
The Mystery of the Mummy's Curse
The Mystery of the Star Ruby
The Stuffed Bear Mystery
The Mystery of Alligator Swamp
The Mystery at Skeleton Point
The Tattletale Mystery
The Comic Book Mystery
The Great Shark Mystery
The Ice Cream Mystery
The Midnight Mystery

The Mystery in the Fortune Cookie
The Black Widow Spider Mystery
The Radio Mystery
The Mystery of the Runaway Ghost
The Finders Keepers Mystery
The Mystery of the Haunted Boxcar
The Clue in the Corn Maze
The Ghost of the Chattering Bones
The Sword of the Silver Knight
The Game Store Mystery
The Mystery of the Orphan Train
The Vanishing Passenger
The Giant Yo-Yo Mystery
The Creature in Ogopogo Lake
The Rock 'n' Roll Mystery
The Secret of the Mask
The Seattle Puzzle
The Ghost in the First Row
The Box That Watch Found
A Horse Named Dragon
The Great Detective Race
The Ghost at the Drive-In Movie
The Mystery of the Traveling Tomatoes
The Spy Game
The Dog-Gone Mystery
The Vampire Mystery
Superstar Watch
The Spy in the Bleachers
The Amazing Mystery Show
The Clue in the Recycling Bin
Monkey Trouble
The Zombie Project
The Great Turkey Heist
The Garden Thief
The Boardwalk Mystery

THE BOARDWALK MYSTERY

created by
GERTRUDE CHANDLER WARNER

ALBERT WHITMAN & Company
Chicago, Illinois

Library of Congress Cataloging-in-Publication Data

Warner, Gertrude Chandler
The boardwalk mystery / by Gertrude Chandler Warner ;
[interior illustrations by Robert Dunn].
p. cm. — (The Boxcar children mysteries ; 131)
Summary: "The Aldens visit the shore in New Jersey and help out at an
amusement pier that is rumored to be unsafe"—Provided by publisher.
ISBN 978-0-8075-0802-2 (hardcover)—ISBN 978-0-8075-0803-9 (pbk.)
[1. Mystery and detective stories 2. Brothers and sisters—Fiction. 3. Orphans—
Fiction. 4. Beaches—Fiction. 5. Amusement parks—Fiction. 6. New Jersey—Fiction.]
I. Dunn, Robert, ill. II. Title.
PZ7.W244Bnm 2013
[Fic]—dc23
2012020161

10 9 8 7 6 5 4 3 2 1 LB 17 16 15 14 13

Cover illustration © 2013 by Tim Jessell.
Interior illustrations by Robert Dunn.

For information about Albert Whitman & Company,
visit our web site at www.albertwhitman.com.

Contents

CHAPTER   PAGE

1. Grandfather's Surprise   1
2. Lost in the House of Mirrors   15
3. A List of Clues   28
4. Benny Disappears   40
5. Benny Gets Hurt   55
6. Zombie on the Beach   64
7. A Mysterious Find in the Ocean   76
8. A Castle on the Beach   88
9. Violet Has an Idea   199
10. An Accidental Confession   111

THE BOARDWALK MYSTERY

CHAPTER 1

Grandfather's Surprise

Henry shut down the lawn mower and suddenly everything was very quiet in Grandfather's front yard. It was so hot that the birds were not chirping. Henry looked up at the blazing sun. He wiped his brow. Then he looked around the yard. Something was missing.

"Benny!" Henry called out to his little brother. "Where are you?"

Just then, ten-year-old Violet came out onto the front porch.

1

"Have you seen Benny?" Henry asked.

"No, I haven't," Violet said. "I thought he was helping you to cut the lawn."

Only six years old, Benny was the youngest of the four Alden children. Henry, Violet, and their sister Jessie took very good care of their little brother. The Aldens were orphans. When their parents died, they ran away from home and lived for a while in an abandoned boxcar in the woods. Their grandfather found them and brought them to live with him in his big house in Greenfield.

The screen door opened and twelve-year-old Jessie stepped outside. She was carrying a pitcher of lemonade and a plate of cookies.

"Benny is missing," Violet said.

Jessie looked around the yard. For a minute, she was concerned. Then she smiled. She saw something that Henry and Violet had not seen. "Watch this," Jessie said to Violet.

Jessie leaned over the porch rail. "Who wants chocolate chip cookies and lemonade?" she shouted.

Henry, Jessie, and Violet soon saw two

little white sneakers dangling from within the tree on Grandfather's front lawn.

"I do!" came a small voice from behind the leaves. "But I can't get down!"

Henry rushed to the tree and caught Benny just as his brother slid from the bottom branch.

"Thanks, Henry!" Benny rushed straight to the porch. "Are there any cookies left? I'm starved!"

Benny was small, but he was famous for his big appetite.

"What were you doing in the tree?" Henry asked. "I thought you were raking up the grass for me."

"I'm sorry, Henry," Benny said. His shoulders slumped. "It's just that it is so hot. I was melting. The tree looked like the coolest place to be. But I was sweating even in the tree. It is hot everywhere!"

Mrs. McGregor, the Aldens' housekeeper, appeared in the doorway. "Benny Alden!" she cried. "Look at all that dirt on your clothes! What happened? Are you okay?"

Benny looked down at his shirt. He tried to brush the dirt off. "I climbed the tree, Mrs. McGregor! I'm tall enough to reach the bottom branch!"

Mrs. McGregor smiled. "I hope you are tall enough to reach the sink. You need to wash up before you have any cookies."

"I'll take him inside," Henry said. "I need to wash up, too."

"Be quick," Mrs. McGregor said. "I was just coming out to tell you that your grandfather called. He will be home soon and he has some exciting news for you children."

Henry and Benny cleaned up and quickly joined their sisters on the front porch.

Jessie took a long drink of lemonade. She was wearing a light summer dress and fanning herself with a magazine. "What do you think the news could be?" she asked.

Violet patted her face with a cool cloth. Her cheeks were bright red from the heat. Even the purple ribbon in her hair seemed to droop. Purple was Violet's favorite color. "I don't know, Jessie. But I can't wait to find out!"

"We'll soon know," Henry said. "Here comes Grandfather now."

A big car drove up the long driveway. Grandfather waved at the children.

"Grandfather!" Benny jumped up. "What is the exciting news? Did you bring ice cream?"

Grandfather laughed. "That would have been a good idea, Benny, but I do not have ice cream. I wanted to tell you that I have to go out of town for a business meeting. Would you like to come with me?"

"We'd be happy to come, Grandfather," Jessie said. "Where is the meeting?"

"It is in a town called Oceanside in New Jersey. I have an old friend who recently moved to Oceanside. He has a big house right on the beach and he invited all of us to be his guests."

Benny dropped his cookie and ran into the house.

"Benny!" Jessie called. "Wait! Where are you going?"

"To pack my suitcase!" Benny called.

Everyone laughed and followed Benny inside.

It wasn't long until their bags were packed and everyone was settled comfortably into Grandfather's car for the long ride.

Violet was the first to guess when they got close to Oceanside. She saw seagulls flying above. Some were perched on the top rails of a bridge that the car was approaching. The bridge crossed over a lot of water.

"The bay is beautiful," Violet said.

"I like it here already," Benny said. "And it smells good."

Grandfather lowered all the windows in the car. He took a deep breath. "I also like that smell, Benny. It is the salt air."

All at once, Benny cried out. He pointed out the car window. "Look! Is that the top of a Ferris wheel?"

Violet looked off into the distance. "I think you are right, Benny. Is there an amusement park in Oceanside, Grandfather?"

Grandfather smiled. "In Oceanside, it is called an amusement pier. And there are several of them."

Benny bounced in his seat. "There is more than one? Cool!"

"Why is it called an amusement pier?" Jessie asked.

"I will show you." Grandfather turned the car onto Ocean Avenue. "See the boardwalk over there?"

Henry, Jessie, Violet, and Benny stared. They had never seen anything like the boardwalk. It was made out of wood planks. It was like a street, but it was raised above the ground, and there were no cars. People were strolling along it. It seemed to go on for miles.

"Does it go on forever?" Benny asked.

Grandfather laughed. "The boardwalk is several miles long, but it does not go on forever. You cannot see from here, but on the other side of the boardwalk are the beach and the ocean."

Just as Grandfather finished speaking, he pulled the car up beside a large, old house on Ocean Avenue. A pretty porch with wooden rails circled the house. Potted flowers hung from the top of the porch and swayed in the cool ocean breeze.

"Hello!" called a friendly voice. "Welcome!" A tall man with short brown hair hurried down the wooden steps. He shook Grandfather's hand. "It's so good to see you, James," he said.

Grandfather introduced his friend to the children. The man's name was Carl Hanson.

"We're very pleased to meet you, Mr. Hanson," Jessie said.

Violet was still gazing at the old house. "And your home is very lovely," she said.

Benny looked past the house. He started to jump up and down. "I see it! I see it!" he cried. "There's the ocean! It's right in your front yard, Mr. Hanson! Right over those dunes. This is way cooler than sitting in Grandfather's tree."

After everyone had unpacked and was settled into their rooms, Mr. Hanson invited his guests outside onto the porch. The porch sat up high on the second story of the house and looked out over the dunes, the boardwalk, and the beach.

Benny was too excited to sit. He hung over the rail and stared out at the waves crashing onto the beach. People strolled past on the boardwalk. Some pushed babies in coaches or licked dripping ice cream cones. There were lots of shops and arcades. And Benny could now see the big Ferris wheel slowly turning against the sky.

Violet came and stood beside Benny to see all the sights. They noticed one girl walking very slowly across the beach. She was staring at her phone. She was wearing shorts and a T-shirt and there was an odd spray of red dots on her shoes. Violet and Benny watched the girl walk all the way up to the Hanson's porch.

"Wendy!" Mr. Hanson cried. "What are you doing here?

The girl looked up. She seemed surprised to see the Aldens. She had long blond hair and her green T-shirt said "Hanson's Amusements" on the front.

"The roller coaster is broken again," the girl said. "I hurried here to tell you."

Benny looked at Violet. He was confused.
Wendy had not been hurrying at all.

Mr. Hanson sighed. "How could that be?
I just had it fixed yesterday! Did Will look
at it? Is anyone stuck on the ride? Who
is working in the ticket booth while you
are gone?"

Wendy shrugged. "I don't know." She went
back to looking at her phone.

Mr. Hanson introduced Wendy as his
daughter. Then he jumped up. He ran his
hand through his hair and walked back

and forth on the porch. "I'm sorry to be so distracted," he said to the Aldens. "But I am a little worried. I recently bought one of the amusement piers on the boardwalk."

Benny's eyes grew wide. He pointed toward the Ferris wheel. "Do you mean the amusement park down there? That is so cool!"

Mr. Hanson nodded. "That's the one, Benny. But it hasn't been as much fun as I thought. I used to work there during the summers back when I was a teenager and visiting with my grandparents. Those were some of the best summers of my life. So when I heard that the amusement pier was up for sale, I bought it and moved my family here from Colorado."

"But why isn't it fun?" Benny asked.

Mr. Hanson ran his hand across his forehead. "Nothing is going right. The rides keep breaking down. The tickets have gone missing. One day there was a nest of bees in the cotton candy machine! Last week someone even painted smiley faces on the walls of the haunted house. It took me hours to clean it up."

"How terrible!" Jessie said.

"And now the roller coaster is broken again. And it is my most popular ride. Two of my employees have already called in sick. It's going to be such a busy night. I don't know what I am going to do."

"We could help," Jessie said.

"Yes," Henry agreed. "I'd be happy to do any small repairs you might need."

"Henry is really good at fixing things," Benny said.

Mr. Hanson looked very surprised. "But you children are on a holiday. I could not ask you to do all that work."

"My grandchildren are very helpful," Grandfather said. "They don't mind hard work."

Wendy glared at the Aldens.

"Well," Mr. Hanson said. "If you are sure you don't mind, I really could use the help."

"I guess you don't need me anymore," she said to her father. "I'm going to go take a nap." Wendy turned to the Aldens. "Have fun, kids. But you better watch out for old Mrs. Reddy. She's prowling around again." Wendy stomped into the house and slammed the screen door.

Mr. Hanson sighed again. "Don't pay attention to that, kids. Mrs. Reddy is the lady who used to own the amusement pier. Even though she sold the pier to me, she can't seem to stay away."

"Then why did she sell it to you?" asked Benny.

"She told me she was ready to retire," Mr.

Hanson said. "Running an amusement pier is a lot of work. But now I think she misses it. She does not like any of the changes that I have made to the pier. She complains that I am doing everything wrong. And she gets into arguments with Bob Cooke."

"Does he work for you, too?" Benny asked.

"Oh, no, Benny. Bob does not work for me. He owns the amusement pier next to mine. It's a long story." Mr. Hanson rubbed his hands together. "I better get going. Why don't you kids have a snack and relax for a little bit after your trip? I'll see you later on tonight." Mr. Hanson hurried away

"What a shame," Grandfather said. "Owning the amusement pier has always been Carl's dream."

Jessie stared toward the tall Ferris wheel. "It sounds like his dream is turning into a nightmare."

CHAPTER 2

Lost in the House of Mirrors

After Grandfather left for his meeting, Henry, Jessie, Violet, and Benny cleaned up the snack plates from the porch.

The children could hear Wendy walking back and forth in a room upstairs. The old floorboards creaked. She was talking to someone on her phone. Soon she began to shout angrily.

"We should probably leave now," Jessie said. "It is not right for us to eavesdrop."

Henry agreed. The children quietly left the

house and began walking on the boardwalk toward the amusement pier. The sun was warm, but a fresh ocean breeze blew through their hair.

"Why was Wendy shouting?" Benny asked. "Who was she was talking to?"

"I don't know, Benny," Jessie said. "Something must have upset her."

"I hope she is all right," Violet said.

Benny began running ahead. "Wow! Look at all these shops!" he cried, pointing to the long rows of stores along the boardwalk. There was an ice cream shop with thirty different flavors. Next to it was a candy store. In the window a machine moved back and forth, pulling saltwater taffy. A souvenir store displayed colorful shells, beach balls, postcards, and paddleball games.

"Can I buy a souvenir?" Benny cried. He darted toward the store.

"Benny, watch out!" Jessie cried.

Violet dashed toward her brother.

"Watch the tramcar, please! Watch the tramcar, please!"

Violet grabbed Benny's shoulders and pulled him back just in time. Benny turned, wide-eyed. A long yellow vehicle, like a train on rubber wheels, came to a slow stop right where Benny had just been standing!

Henry and Jessie rushed to their brother. "Are you all right, Benny?" Jessie asked.

Benny was shaken. He looked like he might cry.

A girl with dark hair jumped from behind the wheel. "Is everyone all right?" she asked.

"Yes. We're sorry for holding you up," Henry said.

"Oh, that's okay," said the girl. "It happens all the time. People are looking at the ocean or the shops and they do not see me coming. But I drive very slowly. I have never hit anyone!"

"But why are you driving a train on the boardwalk?" Benny asked.

The girl laughed. "It does look like a train. But this is the tramcar. The boardwalk is very long. Sometimes people get tired of walking. The tramcar takes them on a nice ride so they can rest. Why don't you hop aboard?"

"Really?" Benny turned toward Jessie. "Can we?" he asked.

Jessie smiled. "I don't see why not," she said.

The tramcar driver introduced herself. Her name was Leslie. She showed Benny a button next to the steering wheel. Every time she pushed the button, a tape played over a loudspeaker. "Watch the tramcar, please! Watch the tramcar, please!"

"So, you see, it wasn't just you, Benny," Leslie explained. "Plenty of people do not notice the tramcar coming. They are too busy having fun on the boardwalk! That is why I have this recording. It saves my voice!"

Suddenly, the children heard a loud banging. An older lady seated in the last car of the tram was banging her cane against the side. "Let's get a move on!" she shouted. "What is going on up there, Leslie?"

"We'll be starting in a minute, Mrs. Reddy," Leslie called. "Just picking up a few passengers."

"Tell them to stop standing around and get into a seat!" Mrs. Reddy called.

"We're very sorry," Jessie said.

Henry, Jessie, Violet, and Benny quickly climbed aboard. Benny leaned from his seat so that he would not miss a thing. Suddenly, he felt a tap on his shoulder. The old woman

was poking him with her cane.

"Better not lean too far out, boy," she said. "Do you want to fall out?"

Jessie had her arm around Benny's shoulder. She knew Benny would not fall out. "He is safe, thank you," she said.

Benny turned to face the old woman. "We're going to Hanson's Amusement Pier!" he said. "They have rides there!"

The old woman folded her hands over her cane. "Well, maybe it is called Hanson's now. But it used to be called Reddy's. It was called Reddy's for fifty years. Stupid to change the name, if you ask me."

"Watch the tramcar, please! Watch the tramcar, please!" Leslie turned on the recording to warn a lady who was walking too close to the tramcar. The lady had a large camera and she was taking pictures of the boardwalk.

"Who built the amusement pier? The Reddy family, that's who! Who made it a big success? The Reddy family! Carl Hanson will ruin the place. He doesn't know what he is doing." The old woman scowled.

Just then, Leslie stopped the tramcar. "This is Hanson's Amusement Pier, kids. Do you need to get off?"

"Yes, thank you," Jessie said.

The children jumped down from the tramcar and thanked Leslie for the ride.

"Any time," Leslie said. Then she lowered her voice. "Don't mind old Mrs. Reddy," she whispered. "She is still upset about why she had to sell her amusement pier." Leslie waved good-bye, and the tramcar began to roll off down the boardwalk.

Jessie held Benny's hand. She wondered what had happened that made Mrs. Reddy sell her pier. The old woman seemed very unhappy about her decision.

Benny waited for the tramcar to safely pass, then let go of Jessie's hand and ran across the boardwalk to the pier. "Look!" he cried. "This is it!"

The name "Hanson's Amusement Pier" flashed in red letters high over Benny's head. There was a log flume that splashed water on the passengers. A tall roller coaster with lots of twists and turns made the boards under Benny's feet rumble. A scary monster with green eyes looked out from the top floor of the haunted house. There was even a giant slide and swings that flew round and round out over the beach below.

"I'll go ask where we can find Mr. Hanson," Henry said. He walked toward the ticket booth. For a moment, he was confused. He thought he saw Wendy's face in the booth window. But she could not have been there. Then he realized that it was a boy in the booth. The boy had the same blond hair and blue eyes as Wendy. He also had the same unhappy look on his face.

"Excuse me," Henry said to the boy. "But would you please tell me where I can find Mr. Hanson?"

The boy opened a door and walked out of the booth. He was a little taller than Henry and he looked a few years older. "Are you those Alden kids?" he asked.

"Yes," Henry replied. He introduced his sisters and brother.

"I'm Will Hanson," the boy said.

"You look just like Wendy!" Benny said.

"We do look alike," Will said. "Wendy and I are twins. My father is in the shed at the back of the pier."

"Thanks," Henry said. "We promised we would stop by."

Will shrugged. "Suit yourself. If I were you kids, I wouldn't hang around this pier. I would go relax on the beach. I'm sure it is much more fun." Will went back into the booth and closed the door behind him.

Henry, Jessie, Violet, and Benny walked back toward the shed at the end of the pier. There, Mr. Hanson was painting something on a white cloth. He smiled when he saw the Aldens.

"Hello! Welcome to my workshop." Mr. Hanson had a big smile on his face. He held up the white cloth. "What do think?" he asked.

Benny cocked his head. "What is it?" he asked.

Mr. Hanson's shoulders slumped. "It is supposed to be a ghost. Someone stole the family of ghosts from my haunted house. I need to replace them. But I guess I am not doing a very good job."

"Violet is a terrific artist!" Benny said. "She can draw anything!"

Violet blushed. "I do like to draw, Mr. Hanson," she said. "If you would like, I could make a family of ghosts for you."

Mr. Hanson jumped up. "That would be great!" he said. He showed Violet all the materials that he had bought for the job. "Now I can go fix the motorcycles."

"You fix motorcycles?" Benny asked.

"Not real ones," Mr. Hanson said. "I have a motorcycle ride for children. They can sit on small motorcycles and pretend that they are riding them. But two nights ago, someone took all the handles off the motorcycles. I had to order new handles. Now I have to screw all the new handles back on to the motorcycles."

"I can do that for you," Henry offered.

"Thank you so much," Mr. Hanson said. "Now I just have to fix up the house of mirrors and the boat ride."

"What's a house of mirrors?" Benny asked.

Mr. Hanson smiled. "Have you never been in one? It is a lot of fun. It is a maze where all of the walls are made of glass. It is fun to try to find your way out. But first I need to clean it up. Someone has written all over the walls."

"That's terrible!" Jessie said. "Who would do such a thing?"

Mr. Hanson shrugged. "Probably one of my customers. It is a big amusement pier. I cannot watch every ride at the same time. Some customers are not very respectful. They break things when I am not looking. I don't know why they do that."

"You should fix the boat ride, Mr. Hanson," Jessie said. "Benny and I will clean the house of mirrors."

Benny and Jessie grabbed some sponges and a bucket of soapy water and headed to the house of mirrors. Just before they got there, a man rudely bumped into Jessie and she almost spilled the bucket of soapy water.

"Watch where you are going!" the man shouted.

"Excuse me," Jessie said. "But I believe you bumped into me."

The man was tall with dark, curly hair. He looked down at Jessie. "Maybe I did. I don't know. Do you kids work here?"

"We are helping out," Jessie said. "Is there something that you need?"

Just then, Mrs. Reddy walked toward them, shaking her cane. "Get off this pier, Bob Cooke!" she shouted.

The man rolled his eyes, but he did not move. "You don't own the pier anymore, Mrs. Reddy. You can't order me off."

Mrs. Reddy banged her cane into the boardwalk. "You don't belong here!"

"You don't, either," he said. Mr. Cooke pointed to Jessie and Benny. "Do you see that Carl is making little children work for him now? He is desperate."

Jessie's face flushed with anger. Before she could answer, Mrs. Reddy did. "These are just kids helping out. But Carl Hanson is ruining this amusement pier."

Mr. Cooke smiled. "I know," he answered.

"He will be out of business by the end of the summer. And then I will buy the amusement pier. I will own more amusements than anyone on this boardwalk."

"You will never own this pier!" Mrs. Reddy said.

"Come on, Benny," Jessie said. She felt uncomfortable listening to the two adults arguing. Jessie and Benny walked into the house of mirrors.

"Wow!" Benny cried. "Look at it!"

There were walls of glass as far as Jessie and Benny could see. Every time they turned one corner, another wall of glass was in front of them. It was hard to know which way to go. Jessie set her bucket down. She was about to ask Benny for a sponge when she noticed that he was gone!

"Benny!" Jessie cried. "Where are you?" But there was no answer. Jessie began to run through the maze of mirrors. Several times she banged hard into a glass wall that she did not see. She could not find her way out!

CHAPTER 3

A List of Clues

Jessie stood very still for a moment and listened. She could hear footsteps from somewhere inside the maze. She tried calling to Benny again, but he did not answer. She put her hands in front of her face and felt her way around the glass walls. Then, suddenly, it became easier. Someone had splashed a red liquid on the glass. Now Jessie could see where she was going. Soon, she saw black scribbles on the glass walls, too. And she saw words. "This way out" was written on one wall. Arrows pointed the way. "This is a stupid ride," read another wall. Finally, Jessie saw "Go to Cooke's Amusement Pier. It is much more fu—" The sentence was not finished.

Jessie looked down. A black marker was laying on the ground. She picked it up and put it in her pocket. She felt a tap on her back and she jumped!

"Benny!" Jessie cried. "Where were you?"

Benny rubbed his forehead. "I was just trying out the maze, Jessie. It is hard. I ran right into the glass walls two times. But then I saw the red paint. I was going to come back to you."

"Didn't you hear me calling to you?" Jessie asked.

"No," Benny said. "I got too far away. There was someone else in the maze with us. I thought it was you. But it wasn't. The person was writing on the walls. The person saw me coming and ran away."

Jessie pulled the marker out of her pocket. "I found this," she said. "Did you see who was writing on the walls?"

"No," Benny said. "I could not see the person. There were too many glass walls in the way. But the person was wearing blue pants. I could see that."

Jessie and Benny carefully retraced their steps. They found the bucket with the soapy water. They worked hard and rubbed off all the red splashes and all the black words from the maze walls. When they finished, they walked back toward the shed.

They passed Henry. He was just screwing on the last handle on a motorcycle. "That should do it," he said. Then he joined Jessie and Benny.

"Wow! Look at what Violet has done!" Benny cried as they arrived at the shed.

A family of scary-looking ghosts stood on the table.

"Listen to this," Violet said. She pushed the button on a recorder. Benny jumped and grabbed Jessie's hand. The frightening wail of ghosts filled the shed.

"It's just pretend, Benny," Violet said. "Mr. Hanson recorded it. The ghost sounds will play when customers ride through the haunted house. We are going to set up the ghosts soon."

"You kids have been working very hard," Mr. Hanson said. "Why don't you go get some dinner on the boardwalk? We can set up the ghosts in the haunted house when you get back. There is a wonderful pizza place called Mack's. I will write down the directions for you."

Mr. Hanson walked toward the ticket booth.

Will was there. He looked bored. There were no customers buying tickets yet.

"Will, where is the black marker? I need to write something down for the Aldens," Mr. Hanson said.

Will stood up. He patted the counter. "I don't know. It was here earlier. I guess someone took it."

Jessie suddenly remembered something. She pulled the marker from her pocket that she had found in the house of mirrors. "I have a marker," she said. "You may have this one if you like."

Will narrowed his eyes at Jessie. "That looks just like our marker." He turned toward his father. "You better watch these kids, Dad. You don't know very much about them."

Jessie's face flushed. "I found that marker in the house of mirrors," she said.

Mr. Hanson held up his hands. "Will, please don't say such things. I trust the Aldens."

"Maybe you shouldn't." Will walked out of the ticket booth. He pointed to Jessie and Benny. "I saw those two talking to Bob Cooke and Mrs. Reddy earlier today. Who knows what they were plotting?" Then Will stomped off down the boardwalk. Benny noticed something odd about Will's sneakers as Will walked away. They had the same red splatters on them as Wendy's shoes.

"Don't mind Will," Mr. Hanson said. "He and Wendy have had a hard time moving here to Oceanside. They miss their friends in Colorado. They haven't been themselves lately."

Henry, Jessie, Violet, and Benny headed

down the boardwalk toward Mack's. Jessie was still upset at Will's accusation. The children found Mack's without any problem. The smell of baking pizza wafted over the boardwalk.

"Hello!" called a friendly man in a white apron. "Are you the Aldens? Carl Hanson just called to tell me how hard you have worked today. I saved the best booth for you."

"Thank you so much," Jessie said.

The children slid into a booth. On the side of the restaurant that faced the ocean, there was no wall. A fresh ocean breeze blew through the restaurant.

"I'm sorry that Will accused you," Henry said to Jessie and Benny. "That was wrong of him."

Jessie explained how she and Benny had run into Mr. Cooke. She told Henry and Violet about the argument between Mr. Cooke and Mrs. Reddy.

"Do you think Mr. Cooke or Mrs. Reddy could be causing the problems at Hanson's Amusement Pier?" Violet asked.

"It is possible," Jessie said. "Mr. Cooke wants Mr. Hanson to fail. Mr. Cooke wants to buy Hanson's Amusement Pier so that he can own the most amusements on the boardwalk."

Jessie pulled out a notepad. When the Aldens were faced with a mystery, Jessie liked to keep notes. Many times her notes helped solve the mystery. Jessie wrote Mr. Cooke's name in her notepad. She wrote down the things he had said.

"What about Mrs. Reddy?" asked Benny. "She seems angry at Mr. Hanson."

"That's true, Benny," Jessie said. She added Mrs. Reddy's name to her list. "Mrs. Reddy thinks that Mr. Hanson is ruining the amusement pier. The amusement pier was owned by her family for a long time. She seems to want it back."

"I don't understand why she sold it," Violet said.

"She told Mr. Hanson that she wanted to retire," Henry said.

Jessie continued to write. She looked thoughtful. "But Leslie, the lady from the tramcar, said that Mrs. Reddy was upset about *why* she had to sell the amusement pier."

"That's true," Henry agreed. "I wonder what she meant by that."

Just then Mack delivered a large, hot pizza with bubbling cheese to their table. A boy followed him with four glasses of ice-cold lemonade.

"Wow!" Benny cried. "This pizza looks great! I think I could eat the whole thing by myself."

Mack introduced the boy with the lemonade as his son, Hunter. Hunter had soft brown hair and a dark tan. He looked like he was a few years older than Henry.

"Pleased to meet you," Hunter said. "Are you kids here on vacation?"

"Yes," Henry answered. "And we're helping out at Hanson's Amusement Pier, as well."

"That's very nice of you," Hunter said. "Mr. Hanson can use all the help he can get. His kids, Will and Wendy, don't seem to like to work. And they're not very friendly."

Mack shook his head. "They're just having

a hard time. They moved here from far away and left all their friends behind."

"Then they should make new friends here," Hunter said. "There are lots of great kids in Oceanside."

"Maybe you should invite them surfing with you," Mack suggested.

"Surfing? Are you a surfer?" Benny asked. "I would like to surf too!"

Hunter smiled. "I do like to surf. You might be a little small to surf, Benny. But I could teach you how to boogie board."

Benny hopped out of his seat. He turned to Jessie. "Can I boogie board? Please? Can I go now?"

Hunter laughed. "I'm sorry, Benny, but I have to work right now. But maybe I can take you another day."

"Thanks!" Benny said.

The children began eating the delicious pizza. Benny was so excited about boogie boarding that he almost dropped his slice of pizza. Some of the red sauce squirted onto his T-shirt. Violet tried to clean it off with her napkin.

"It won't come off, Benny," Violet said. "We'll have to wash it when we get home."

Benny looked down at the red stains on his shirt. It reminded him of something. "Now my shirt looks like Will's and Wendy's shoes," he said.

Jessie thought for a minute. Benny was right. She did remember seeing red stains on the twins' shoes. She pulled out her notepad. She added Will's and Wendy's names to her list. She told Henry and Violet about the red liquid that was spilled on the walls of the house of mirrors. Benny explained about the words written in black marker. He also told how he had seen someone in blue pants running away through the maze.

"Jessie," Henry said. "Is that the marker you found in the house of mirrors?"

Jessie looked down at the marker in her hand. "Yes, it is. I suppose that I was so upset at Will's accusation, I forgot to put it back on the counter."

"Look at what is printed on the side of the

marker," Henry said.

Jessie turned the marker on its side. She read out loud, "Captain Cooke's Amazing Amusement Pier."

The children were surprised.

"I have another clue for your notepad, Jessie," Benny said. "Mr. Cooke was wearing blue pants."

"You are a good detective, Benny," Violet said. "But I think that Will was also wearing blue pants today."

Jessie wrote all the information down in the notepad.

"It's getting late," Henry said. "We promised Mr. Hanson that we would come back to help set up Violet's ghosts in the haunted house."

"Yes," Jessie agreed. "But perhaps we should take a look around Captain Cooke's pier first."

CHAPTER 4

Benny Disappears

Captain Cooke's pier was smaller than Hanson's, but there were many exciting rides there.

"Look!" Benny cried. He pointed to a very large pirate ship. The ship rocked high into the air, back and forth.

There were also games where people could win prizes. One booth had a big wall filled with balloons. People threw darts and tried to pop the balloons.

"Can I try that?" asked Benny. "It won't take long. Please?"

Henry laughed. "Sure, Benny," he said. "Let's see if you can win a prize."

Henry paid the man in the booth. The man handed Benny three darts.

Benny rubbed his hands together. He was excited. He reached back and threw his first dart very hard, but he missed. The dart stuck into the corkboard wall.

"Almost, Benny!" Violet said. "You'll get the next one."

Benny took aim again. He threw his second dart and it hit a small yellow balloon. But the balloon did not pop!

The man in the booth whispered to Benny. Benny looked confused, then he nodded. He aimed for a big red balloon down in the corner. He let the dart fly. It hit the red balloon and there was a loud pop!

"You did it, Benny!" Violet cried.

A green ticket fluttered to the ground. The man in the booth picked it up and handed it to Benny. "Looks like you are a winner!" he said. The man smiled and gave Benny a long rubber snake.

"Cool!" Benny showed his snake to his brother and sisters. "It looks so real! Do you think I can scare Grandfather with it?"

Henry laughed. "Maybe you can."

The children were so busy looking at Benny's prize that they did not see Mr. Cooke walk toward them. He was carrying a folder and some papers. He stopped at the dart-throwing booth.

"I see you have come to the better amusement pier," Mr. Cooke said. "Did you get tired of all the broken rides at Hanson's?" Mr. Cooke spoke very loudly. He spoke like he was an actor on a stage. People on the boardwalk turned and looked at him.

"Not at all," Jessie said. "And the rides at Hanson's are not broken. We are just on our way there right now."

The man in the dart booth was counting money. He handed the bills to Mr. Cooke. Mr. Cooke took a paper out of his folder.

"Be careful over at Hanson's," Mr. Cooke said. "They have been having so much trouble with their rides, it might not be very safe over there."

"We are sure that it is perfectly safe," Henry said.

The man in the dart booth held out his hand. "I need a receipt for the money, Mr. Cooke," he said.

Mr. Cooke put his hand into each of his pockets. "I know," he said. "But I can't find my marker."

"Is this your marker?" Jessie asked.

Mr. Cooke took the marker from Jessie's hand. He started to nod, but then he stopped, as if he was remembering something. He looked at the marker, then stared at Jessie. "There are a hundred markers with my name on them on this boardwalk," he said. "I give them out for free. They are a good advertisement. You can find them everywhere."

"Well, I found your marker at Hanson's pier," Jessie said.

Mr. Cooke signed the receipt for the man in the dart booth. "I'm not surprised you found it at Hanson's. Like I said, those markers are everywhere."

Mr. Cooke handed the marker back to Jessie. "You can keep this as a souvenir," he said. "It is probably not the one I lost." Then he quickly walked away.

The Aldens were running late. They hurried toward Hanson's pier. But very soon they heard a familiar recording. "Watch the tramcar, please! Watch the tramcar, please!"

"Hello, kids!" Leslie waved from behind the wheel of the bright yellow tram. "Why don't you jump aboard? Are you headed to Hanson's?"

"Yes," Jessie said. "Thank you so much!"

Henry, Jessie, Violet, and Benny took the front seat right behind Leslie.

"So how do you like Hanson's pier?" Leslie asked.

"It's wonderful," Jessie answered.

Leslie nodded her head. "I knew you would enjoy it. The Reddy family added many great rides over the years. They built it up into the best pier on the boardwalk."

"Do you mean Mrs. Reddy's family?" asked Violet.

Leslie slowed the tramcar. She picked up two families with small children. "That's right, Violet," she said. "Mr. and Mrs. Reddy and their son, Paul, ran the pier for many years."

Violet hesitated. "Do you mind if we ask why the Reddy family sold the pier?"

"Not at all. It is not a secret." Leslie started up the tram again. "Mr. Reddy was a wonderful man. But he died five years ago. Paul helped Mrs. Reddy run the pier. He is a good son and he helped for several years. But Paul did not like working at the amusement pier. He is an engineer. He got an offer for a very good job in California. He moved away and he lives in California with his family."

"It is a shame that he lives so far away," Violet said.

"Mrs. Reddy tried to run the pier by

herself," Leslie said. "But it is a big job and she has a very sore leg. Paul and all of her friends encouraged Mrs. Reddy to sell the pier and to retire. She was very sad that her son did not carry on the family business."

The tramcar slowed to a stop in front of Hanson's pier. "Here we are, kids!" Leslie said. "Have fun tonight!"

The children thanked Leslie and climbed down from the tramcar.

"It must have been very hard for Mrs. Reddy to sell the pier," Violet said.

"Yes," agreed Jessie. "And she must be lonely with her son living so far away."

Benny looked up at all the lights and the spinning rides. "If it were my pier, I would not want to sell it, either!"

The children hurried off to find Mr. Hanson. He was in his workshop carefully placing Violet's ghosts into a large box.

"There you are!" Mr. Hanson said. "How was dinner?"

"It was great!" Benny said. "I ate five pieces of pizza all by myself."

Mr. Hanson's eyes grew wide. He patted Benny's stomach. "Where do you put it all?"

Henry laughed. "That is one mystery we have never been able to solve."

The children followed Mr. Hanson to the haunted house. No one was in line yet. Mr. Hanson placed a sign outside that said "Ride temporarily closed." Then he pushed open a side door and the children followed him into the haunted house. It was very dark.

Benny clutched Jessie's shirt. This was the darkest room he had ever been in! He couldn't even see his own hand!

The children could hear Mr. Hanson struggling with the box. "I can't reach it," he said. "There is a switch on the wall on the left. Can someone turn on the lights?"

Henry felt around in the darkness until his hand felt a switch. He flicked it up. Suddenly, the room was flooded with light. All four Aldens jumped back in fear.

"I'm sorry," Mr. Hanson said. "I should have warned you that we were standing in the zombie room before you turned on the lights."

Jessie was holding her hand over her heart. "Whoever made those zombies did a very good job."

Everyone stared at the rows of tall zombies. They had white faces and red eyes. Their clothes were shabby and their arms were outstretched.

Mr. Hanson set his box on the floor. "It is a good display, isn't it? I made it myself. Watch this." He flipped another switch. The zombies' legs began to move back and forth and the room was filled with a moaning sound. It looked like the zombies were marching straight at the Aldens!

Benny held on to Jessie's hand. "I don't like it in here," he whispered. "It's all pretend," Jessie said. "Don't worry."

Benny stayed very close to Jessie as Mr. Hanson led the children through the haunted house. There was a room with a huge green-faced Frankenstein and a room with a cackling witch on a broom. In the last room, scary jack-o'-lanterns blinked orange. But the rest of the room was empty.

"The ghosts used to be right here." Mr. Hanson pointed to an empty side of the room. There were dark posts lined up next to the wall. But there was nothing else. Mr. Hanson opened the box and everyone carefully removed the ghosts. Mr. Hanson showed the children how to fit the ghosts onto the posts. After the ghosts were screwed on, Violet fluffed out the long white material.

Mr. Hanson turned to Violet. "You did a wonderful job. These ghosts are even better than the ones that were stolen. Why don't you turn on this switch and I will show you what your ghosts can do?"

Violet hit the switch. The posts moved up and down and so did the ghosts! A hidden fan blew air across the ghosts and they seemed to be floating and shimmering in the air.

"Oh my!" Violet cried. "That is very clever! Your machine makes my ghosts move. It really looks like they are flying!"

"Thank you, Violet," said Mr. Hanson.

Suddenly, a loud banging came from the zombie room.

"What could that be?" Mr. Hanson hurried toward the sound. The children followed.

They found Will. He was kicking the wall with his shoe.

"Will! What are you doing?" asked Mr. Hanson.

"I called you, but you didn't answer," Will said. "Linda and Jake are not showing up for work tonight. Mr. Cooke hired them for his pier and he promised to pay them more money. I can't do everything by myself. And I am hungry. I'm leaving to go get some food." Will kicked the wall again.

"Will, can't you just wait until later? I need your help."

Will shrugged. "Sorry, Dad. This whole amusement pier thing is your dream, not mine. It's not my fault that you can't make it work." Will turned and left.

Mr. Hanson sighed. He put his hands deep into his pockets. "Maybe Will is right," he said. "Maybe I just can't make it work. I've worked so hard, but nothing seems to be turning out right. Maybe I should sell the pier and go back to my old job in Colorado."

"But it's not your fault that everything is going wrong," Benny said.

Mr. Hanson looked up, surprised. "What do you mean?"

"Benny is right, Mr. Hanson," Henry said. "You have a wonderful amusement pier. But someone wants you to fail. Someone is trying to ruin you."

Mr. Hanson rubbed his forehead. "Ruin me? But who would do such a thing?" he asked.

"We're not sure yet," Jessie said.

"But whoever it is, is playing a lot of very mean tricks on you," Henry said.

"And you have a truly wonderful amusement pier," Violet added. "You have created some amazing rides."

Mr. Hanson smiled. "Thanks, kids. You are very kind. I guess I shouldn't give up just yet."

He sighed. "Looks like I will be short on help again tonight, though."

"What jobs did Linda and Jake have?" Henry asked.

"Jake runs this haunted house ride," Mr. Hanson said. "And Linda is in charge of the Big Slide. I'll have to close a few of the rides tonight. It's always so hard to choose."

"You don't need to close anything," Henry said. "Benny and I can run the haunted house ride."

"And I would be happy to help out with the Big Slide," Violet said.

"I'll go straight to the ticket booth," Jessie added.

Mr. Hanson smiled. "You are sure that you don't mind?"

"We don't mind at all," Henry said. "It will be fun."

It was late when the amusement pier finally closed. Mr. Hanson, Henry, and Jessie checked that all the rides were safely turned off and locked. Violet and Benny picked up stray wrappers and put them in the trash. When they were done, they climbed onto the dark merry-go-round and each picked a horse. Benny climbed onto a large black horse that looked as though it were galloping.

Violet sat on a white horse that had purple ribbons hanging from its mane.

Benny held the reins of his horse. "Do you think we will get to ride the rides sometime when they are on?"

Violet patted the side of her horse. "I hope so," she said. "I want to try the Big Slide and the roller coaster. I am sure that once Mr. Hanson gets all his problems settled, we can ride the rides."

"And play games, too," Benny said.

"Yes," Violet replied. "That would be fun, too."

Suddenly, Benny slid off his horse. "I'll be right back!" he cried. "I just remembered something!"

"Benny, wait!" Violet called. But it was too late. Benny had disappeared!

CHAPTER 5

Benny Gets Hurt

Violet ran across the amusement pier, but she did not see Benny. A few lights were on here and there, but all the rides and food stands were dark.

"Violet! Is something wrong?" Jessie asked. Jessie, Henry, and Mr. Hanson were locking the gate to the Ferris wheel.

"Have you seen Benny?" Violet asked.

"No," Jessie replied.

Violet explained how Benny had slid from his horse and run away.

Mr. Hanson looked concerned. "Let's split up," he said. "Henry and Jessie, you search the ocean side of the pier. Violet and I will look on the other side. We'll meet up at the ticket booth."

Violet climbed all the way up to the very top of the Big Slide. From the top, she could look down on the whole amusement pier. She could see Henry and Jessie running from ride to ride. She could see Mr. Hanson checking under benches and behind the game booths. But she did not see Benny. Clouds covered the moon, and the beach and the ocean were very dark. Violet worried. What if Benny had run down to the beach and could not find his way?

Out of the corner of her eye, Violet saw something move at the back of the pier. Someone, or something, had just run down the steps and into the blackness of the beach. It looked like the person was carrying something very big.

"Stop!" Violet called. But she was too far. She sat and quickly flew down the Big Slide to the very bottom. She called for Henry, Jessie, and Mr. Hanson. They came running.

Just as Violet was about to tell them what she had seen, loud screaming came from the haunted house! All the lights in the front of the haunted house went on. The cars began to run on the track and bump through the doors. But there were no riders! Everyone rushed toward the ride.

"Was that Benny who screamed?" asked Jessie. "I hope he is all right."

"Don't worry," Mr. Hanson said. "It was not Benny. The screams are part of the ride. Someone has turned it on."

Mr. Hanson quickly found the off switch and shut down the ride. He pushed open the door and Henry, Jessie, and Violet followed him inside.

"Benny!" Jessie cried. "Are you all right?"

Benny sat on the floor in the zombie room. His head was in his hands.

"The zombie hit me," he said. "Then it ran away."

Everyone looked at the platform next to

where Benny sat. The tallest zombie was missing from its stand!

* * *

Back at Mr. Hanson's house, everyone sat out on the deck overlooking the ocean. Mr. Hanson scooped ice cream into bowls.

"Extra chocolate sauce and rainbow sprinkles for Benny," Mr. Hanson said. "How do you feel?"

"I'm fine," Benny said. He lifted an ice pack from his cheek. "It is just a small bump. It hardly hurts at all."

"Can you tell us what happened?" Grandfather asked.

"I won a snake today when I threw darts at a balloon. But when we helped Mr. Hanson set up the ghosts in the haunted house, I left my snake there. I remembered it when I was sitting on the horse on the merry-go-round. I told Violet that I would be right back. I ran to the haunted house to get my snake."

"Wasn't it too dark to find the snake?" Jessie asked.

Benny nodded. "At first it was too dark. But I knew where the light switch was. I turned on the lights and ran to the ghost room. I found my snake. It was sitting right next to the smallest ghost. I picked it up, but just then all the lights went out. I couldn't see anything."

Violet drew in her breath. "You must have been so frightened!"

"I was a little scared," Benny admitted. "But I felt along the walls. I walked into the zombie room. There was a light in there."

"But I don't have any lights just in the zombie room," Mr. Hanson said. "The switch you used turns on all the lights in the haunted house."

"It wasn't that light, Mr. Hanson. It was a small light, like from a cell phone or a little flashlight. Then the giant zombie started to move. He came right off the machine that you built. His arms swung around. One of them hit me in the side of the face. I fell down."

"Where did the zombie go?" asked Henry. "It can't walk. It's not real. And it was not there when we found you."

"I don't know," Benny said. "It was too dark. The little light went off. And then all of a sudden the ride started up and you came and found me."

Just then, everyone heard giggling coming from the beach. But it was too dark to see anyone.

As everyone was finishing their ice cream, Will and Wendy came in the front door. When their father called to them, they walked back toward the deck.

"Where were you tonight?" Mr. Hanson asked. "I sure could have used your help."

Will looked down at his feet.

"We're sorry, Dad," Wendy said. "We went for a long walk after dinner and we lost track of the time."

Wendy played with a string hanging from the bottom of her shirt. Her eyes quickly glanced toward Benny. "Are you okay, little guy?" she asked. "How about I get you some more ice cream?" Wendy asked.

Grandfather smiled. "Benny never says no to ice cream."

Wendy carried Benny's bowl into the kitchen.

"Hello up there, Aldens!" A shout came from the boardwalk below.

Mr. Hanson leaned over the rail. "Come on up, Hunter," he said. "We are just having some ice cream. I hope you can join us."

"Sounds great!" Hunter ran up the stairs. "I'm glad I saw the candles flickering on your deck," he said. "I wanted to stop by to see if anyone is up for hitting the beach tomorrow morning."

Benny jumped out of his chair. "Are you going to teach me how to boogie board?"

Hunter laughed. "That's the first thing I am going to do. But it won't take long. You'll figure it out quick."

"You children have been an enormous help. You should go and enjoy the beach tomorrow," Mr. Hanson said.

Benny clapped his hands. Wendy came back out onto the deck and handed Benny another heaping bowl of ice cream. "Wow!" Benny said. "This is the best night ever!"

Will and Wendy turned to leave the deck. Hunter called to them.

"Do you want to come tomorrow, too?" Hunter asked. "There will be lots of kids there. We always have a good time. Do you like to surf?"

Will hesitated. He folded his arms and leaned against the door frame.

"Thanks, but we don't surf," Wendy said. Then she sighed. "But we used to ski when we lived in Colorado."

"That's cool," Hunter said. "I've never been skiing. If I teach you to surf this summer, maybe you can teach me how to ski in the winter. I've heard the Pocono Mountains in Pennsylvania have some great slopes. And they are not too far from here."

Wendy smiled. She looked over at Will. Will shrugged his shoulders. "It's a deal," Wendy said. "We'll see you in the morning!"

When Benny awoke, it was early morning. He rushed downstairs and out onto the deck. He wanted to see how big the waves were. He could not wait to swim in the ocean and try out the boogie board that Hunter promised to bring. But when Benny looked toward the beach, he saw something that made his heart beat fast. He stumbled back into the house.

"Henry! Jessie! Violet!" Benny called. "Come quick!"

CHAPTER 6

Zombie on the Beach

Henry, Jessie, and Violet heard Benny's shouting and rushed out onto the deck to find him. Even Grandfather and Mr. Hanson had jumped from their beds. They all stood looking out at the beach. At first, no one knew what to say. The tall zombie, the one that had hit Benny in the face, was standing on the beach, its arms outstretched as though it was marching toward the Hanson's beach house. The sun was rising behind it on the ocean, and the zombie cast a huge shadow across the sand.

"How do you think it got there?" Benny finally whispered. "Do you think it followed me here?"

"No, Benny," Jessie said, putting her hand on her little brother's shoulder. "It is not real. Someone stole the zombie when you were in the haunted house. Then the thief brought the zombie to the beach and left it here."

Violet shook her head. "It is just another mean trick that someone has played on Mr. Hanson."

Mr. Hanson leaned on the deck rail. "I don't know what to do. You children were right. Someone is trying to ruin my business. But who would do such a thing?"

Wendy slid open the screen door and walked out onto the deck. Will was close behind. "Don't worry, Dad. Will and I will put the zombie back."

"What?" Will said. "But I thought . . ."

Wendy shook her head at Will and he stopped talking.

"Thanks, Wendy," Mr. Hanson said. "But you kids should go to the beach and have some fun. This is my problem. I have been asking you and Will to do too much."

"No, Dad," Wendy said. "Will and I can put the zombie in the haunted house. We will go right now. We'll be back in plenty of time for the beach."

"Thanks," Mr. Hanson said. "The key to the haunted house is on my key ring. It is hanging on the hook by the door."

"Will and I have a spare key," Wendy said. "We don't need it."

Will looked down at the zombie. "You have to admit," he said. "It does look kind of funny down there, doesn't it?"

Grandfather smiled. "It certainly gets your attention."

There were a few early morning joggers and walkers on the beach. Some of them were stopping to look at the zombie. They were admiring it.

Violet looked thoughtful. "Mr. Hanson, maybe you could leave the zombie on the beach for a while. We could put a sign on it advertising the amusement pier."

"That's a cool idea!" Benny said. "Violet is a great artist. She could make a really good sign!"

"And we could dress the zombie up!" Wendy said. "What if we put a colorful inflatable swim float over one of his arms? And maybe we could find a big pair of sunglasses to put on his face? I think I saw some of those for sale in the dollar store."

Mr. Hanson nodded his head. "I think it's a great idea!"

Henry, Jessie, Violet, and Benny hurried upstairs to their rooms to find their bathing suits. Mr. Hanson left early to check on the amusement pier and Grandfather went to his business meeting. When the Aldens came back downstairs, Wendy and Will had set the table on the deck with a large platter of blueberry and strawberry waffles. There was even a bowl of whipped cream and a tall container of syrup.

"Wow!" Benny said. "This looks great!"

"Thank you so much," Jessie said. "It is very kind of you."

Wendy smiled. "I hope you like it. It is the least we can do after . . ."

Will poked Wendy in the arm. "You are our guests," Will said. "What Wendy means is that it is the least we can do for our guests. We are going to go find the sunglasses for the zombie. We'll be back soon. Enjoy your breakfast."

The children sat on the deck and ate the delicious breakfast. Soon there was only one waffle left on the big platter that Wendy and Will had set on the table.

"May I have the last waffle?" Benny asked.

"I think you have eaten more waffles than me, Benny," Henry said. "I don't know where you put it all." Henry slid the waffle onto Benny's plate.

"Me either," Benny said. "But my stomach sure does like this breakfast!"

"Does it hurt to eat?" Jessie asked.

Benny touched the side of his face. He had a purple bruise on his right cheek. It was swollen, too. "It hurts a little when I chew," Benny said. "But if I didn't eat, my stomach would hurt more!"

"Who do you think could have done such a thing to Benny?" asked Violet. "It certainly was very mean. He could have been hurt very bad."

Henry poured himself a glass of milk. "I don't know," he said. "And I was quite sure that Mr. Hanson had locked up the haunted house. How did the person get inside? And who turned the ride on?"

Benny wiped a drip of syrup from his chin. "It wasn't locked when I went in," he said. "But I did not turn the ride on. It went on all by itself."

"Someone turned it on," Henry said. "Whoever it was must have sat at the control panel and turned the switches that make the ride start."

"But why would someone do that?" Jessie asked. "Turning the ride on only got our attention. It made us run to the haunted house. The person could have been caught if we were closer and had gotten there quicker."

"That is true," Violet said. She suddenly remembered something. "When I was on the top of the Big Slide, I saw someone or something running down the steps from the pier onto the beach. It was very dark. But it might have been someone carrying the zombie."

"But the ride did not turn on until you were already at the bottom of the Big Slide," Jessie said. "The person could not have run onto the beach, and then snuck back to turn on the ride. We would have seen something."

"That is true," Violet said. "And a person cannot be in two places at the same time. That is a hard mystery to figure out."

While the children discussed the mystery, Violet had finally finished her sign. She turned it around for her sister and brothers to see. "What do you think?" she asked.

"Oh, Violet! It's perfect," Jessie exclaimed.

Henry read the sign aloud. " 'I love the beach. But I can't wait till dark. I am going to go to Hanson's. It is the best amusement pier on the boardwalk!' "

As the children were washing the breakfast dishes, Wendy and Will returned. They had a giant pair of sunglasses, a big yellow duck float, and a colorful beach towel.

"Are you ready to dress up our zombie?" Wendy asked. She handed the float to Benny.

"I'm ready!" Benny ran down the steps and out into the sand. Everyone followed him. Benny gazed up at the giant zombie. "He doesn't look so scary when he is not in the haunted house," he said.

Will agreed. "He looks pretty silly on the beach."

Henry placed the silly sunglasses on the zombie's nose. Benny hung the duck float from the zombie's right arm. Jessie draped the colorful towel over the other arm. A group of people on the beach came over to watch. Many were laughing and calling to their friends.

Violet took her sign and hung it from the zombie's neck.

Two little boys with buckets and shovels ran up to the zombie. "Mommy!" they called. "Come look!"

A woman in a pink bathing suit hurried

to stand behind her boys. "Can we go to Hanson's pier tonight? Pleeeease?" the boys asked.

The mother laughed. "I think we should," she said. "It looks like a fun place!"

Violet noticed a woman taking photographs of the zombie. "This is so great!" the woman said. "Would anyone like a picture taken with this zombie?"

Benny raised his hand. "I would!" he said.

Benny stood beside the zombie with a great big smile on his face. He looked very small next to the big zombie.

The photographer snapped several pictures. When she was done, she handed Jessie her card. "My name is Donna Mancini," she said. "I work for the local paper taking shots for stories. But I also have my own shop.

Jessie looked down at the card. "Thank you very much," she said.

A man wearing a red baseball cap came to admire the zombie with his children. "Is it safe at Hanson's pier?" he asked. "I have heard rumors that they are having lots of trouble with their amusements."

"It is perfectly safe!" Jessie said. "Those rumors are false."

"Mr. Hanson is my dad," Wendy said. "He is a great mechanic and he loves the amusement pier. He would never let anyone get on one of his rides unless it was perfectly safe."

The man folded his arms across his chest. "That is good to know," he said. "But I heard that the roller coaster was broken twice this week."

"It wasn't really broken." Will looked down at his feet before continuing. His face was very red. "Someone accidentally turned off the power. That is all. It is a very fun ride and a great amusement pier. You should come and see for yourself."

"Can we, Dad?" asked the man's children.

The man smiled. "I suppose we can. We'll stop by tonight after dinner."

The children clapped their hands and ran away toward the ocean.

Violet looked up just in time to see Benny racing toward the water as well.

"Benny! Wait!" she called. "Where are you going?"

CHAPTER 7

A Mysterious Find in the Ocean

Hunter waved at the Aldens and at Will and Wendy with his one free hand. He was walking at the edge of the ocean. He had a surfboard and a boogie board under his right arm.

Hunter set his things down in the sand. When Benny reached him, he gave Benny a high five. "Ready to ride the waves?" he asked.

"I sure am!" Benny said.

Henry, Jessie, Violet, and Benny waded

into the ocean. The water was cold, but it was refreshing on such a hot day.

Hunter held the boogie board still. He showed Benny how to grip the front of the board with his hands and wait for a good wave.

"How about this one?" Benny called over the roar as a big whitecap came crashing toward him.

"Go for it!" Hunter yelled.

The wave pushed under Benny's boogie board and shot him toward the beach. He had a very long ride. When it was over, he jumped up and splashed back to Hunter.

"Great job, Benny!" Henry said.

After a long swim, everyone rested in the sand. Wendy had brought a blanket and a cooler full of sandwiches and cold drinks. Hunter's friends joined them.

"Will and Wendy surfed for the first time today," Hunter told his friends. "And they already can catch waves."

Wendy smiled. "We had a good teacher," she said.

"You two should hang out with us," said a boy named Zach. "We come to the beach a lot. And tonight, I am having friends over to my house. Would you like to join us?"

"That sounds like fun," said Will. "But we may have to work. We help out at Hanson's Amusement Pier."

"You work there?" Zach looked down the beach toward the amusement pier. "I heard that place isn't safe. They have been having lots of problems since the new owner took over."

"Who told you that?" asked Jessie.

Zach shrugged. "I don't know. Just people talking. I suppose they are only rumors."

"They are only rumors!" Wendy said. "Hanson's is a great amusement pier. It is very safe."

"I agree with Wendy and Will," said Hunter. The pier is safe. And they should know. Their dad is the owner."

Zach's face turned red. "I'm sorry," he said to Wendy and Will. "I didn't know that your dad was the owner. I didn't mean to say anything against him."

"It's not your fault," Wendy said. "We know that there are false rumors going around."

"Someone is trying to ruin Hanson's," Jessie said.

"Why would someone do that?" asked Tori.

Just then, the lifeguards stood up in their stands and began to blow their whistles. They began to wave at all the swimmers to get out of the ocean. Everyone jumped up and ran to the water's edge to see what was going on.

"There's something in the water!" a woman cried, picking up her toddler.

"Maybe it is a whale!" Benny said.

"It's big, whatever it is," said a man. "There are three strong lifeguards dragging it out of the water."

Suddenly, there were gasps from the crowd. The lifeguards came out of the water and the people all moved out of their way. They were carrying the zombie from the haunted house!

"It's our zombie!" Benny cried.

"This is yours?" asked a dark-haired lifeguard.

Wendy stepped forward. "It is from Hanson's amusement pier," she said. "It belongs to my father."

"How did it get into the water?" asked the lifeguard. "You cannot dump things you do not want in the ocean. That man over there hurt his ankle banging into your zombie. He could not see it beneath the waves."

An older man sat on a blanket in the sand.

He rubbed his ankle as he talked with one of the lifeguards. "I'm fine," the man said. "It's just a little bruise. No need to make a fuss."

"We're so sorry that anyone got hurt," Wendy said. "But we did not dump the zombie in the ocean."

"Someone stole the zombie from the haunted house!" Benny said. "The thief must have put the zombie in the ocean."

The lifeguard looked concerned. "A thief? You should call the police," he said. "They should investigate this."

"No!" Will said quickly. "We do not need the police." He looked at Wendy. "I'm sure it was just a prank."

Wendy nodded. "We'll get to the bottom of it," she said. "We will take the zombie back to the haunted house right now. No one else will get hurt."

Henry, Will, Zach, and Hunter lifted the zombie. Saltwater ran out of holes in his metal shoes and from his eyes.

"It looks like the zombie is crying," Benny said.

"Yes, it does," Wendy agreed. "I feel like crying, too. I feel so bad."

Hunter put his arm around Wendy. "You don't have anything to feel bad about," he said. "This is not your fault."

Wendy looked down at her feet. "In some ways . . ." she began.

"Let's go!" Will said. "Let's get this zombie back right away!"

After the older kids had left with the zombie, Henry, Jessie, Violet, and Benny cleaned up the sandwich wrappers and napkins from their picnic and folded the towels.

"I sure could go for some ice cream," Violet said.

"That's a great idea, Violet," Jessie said.

The children headed up toward the boardwalk.

"Where shall we go?" asked Benny. "There are so many different places!"

Just then, someone called out to them. "Hey, kids!"

Henry, Jessie, Violet, and Benny turned.

Mrs. Reddy was hurrying toward them.

"I heard that Carl Hanson is so upset with the things going on at his amusement pier that he threw his own zombie into the ocean! Isn't that terrible?"

Violet's lips were pressed tightly together while Mrs. Reddy spoke. "Mrs. Reddy," Violet said. "I am sure that Mr. Hanson would not have thrown his own zombie into the ocean."

"Well then, how did it get there?" she asked. "When I ran the amusement pier, none of the ghosts or zombies from my haunted house ever went missing. And none of my property ever ended up in the ocean! And did you hear that some poor man got hurt by the zombie in the ocean? I heard that a wave threw the zombie on top of the man and he got knocked out. He almost drowned!"

"We were there on the beach," Henry replied. "The man only banged his ankle into the zombie under the water."

Mrs. Reddy clicked her tongue. "I don't know," she said. "But that is what I heard. Things are getting bad on that amusement pier. Carl Hanson needs my help. You should tell him that."

Violet looked thoughtful. Mrs. Reddy seemed like a person who liked to be busy and useful.

"Maybe you can help us," Violet said. "We are looking for some ice cream. Do you have a favorite ice cream stand on the boardwalk? Would you have the time to take us there?"

Mrs. Reddy smiled. "Of course!" She linked her arm through Violet's. "Come with me!"

The children walked a half block to Kohr's frozen custard stand. Mrs. Reddy waved to the man behind the counter. "Noah!" she said. "Here are some special guests. These are the Alden children. They have never been to our boardwalk before. I told them that you serve the best ice cream on the whole coast!"

Noah smiled at the compliment. He introduced himself and welcomed the children. While he made their cones, Mrs. Reddy talked nonstop.

"Noah, did you hear that Hanson's zombie

knocked out an old man in the ocean? Poor man almost drowned!"

"I did hear that," Noah said. "Your friend Karen stopped by earlier. She told me. As a matter of fact, there she is now." Noah pointed across the boardwalk.

"Oh yes," Mrs. Reddy said. "I see her. I promised to help her out in her souvenir shop today. Take care, kids. Enjoy your ice cream. And make sure you tell Carl Hanson that he can call me any time he needs advice." Mrs. Reddy hurried off to join her friend.

The children walked toward a bench to eat their ice cream. Benny's cone was vanilla dipped in a hard chocolate shell. Violet got a twist of orange crème and vanilla with rainbow sprinkles. Jessie chose strawberry with chocolate sprinkles and Henry had a thick milkshake.

"This is delicious!" Violet said. She watched the people stroll along the boardwalk while she ate her cone. "Look," she said. "There is the photographer."

Donna Mancini was snapping photos of a

small sandwich shop with a "Grand Opening" banner hanging over the front door. A man in an apron stood under the banner.

"I wonder if that man will get his picture in the paper," Benny said.

"The picture might be for the paper Benny. But it might be for an advertisement for the new store as well." Violet was very interested in photography and she enjoyed watching Ms. Mancini work.

As she watched, Violet saw someone familiar pass by. "Isn't that Bob Cooke?"

Henry, Jessie, and Benny looked across the boardwalk. Mr. Cooke was alone. He was walking quickly. Suddenly, Mrs. Reddy and her friend approached Mr. Cooke. He stopped to talk with them. The children were too far away to hear what he was saying. But Mr. Cooke was smiling.

"What is wrong with Mr. Cooke's pants?" Benny asked.

"I noticed it, too, Benny," Violet said.

Mr. Cooke was wearing a pair of long tan pants. But from the knees down, the pants were very dark. The children also noticed that Mr. Cooke's sneakers left footprints on the boardwalk. It looked as though he had gotten wet somehow.

Mr. Cooke looked up from his conversation with Mrs. Reddy. He saw the Aldens. He looked down at his pants, then quickly hurried away.

CHAPTER 8

A Castle on the Beach

After their ice cream, the children headed
back down to the beach. They arrived just in
time.

"Hurry!" Jessie called.

The tide had come in. Their blanket and
towels were just about to get drenched by the
ocean! The children grabbed their things
and moved them back out of the way of the
water.

"That was close," Jessie said.

"Hunter told me about the tides," Benny

said. "He said that when the tide goes out, I might be able to find some cool seashells to take home as souvenirs."

"It will be fun to look for them," Violet said. "But would you like to help me build a sand castle right now?"

"Sure!" Benny said.

When the castle was finished, the children sat in the sand and waited for the tide to come in.

Violet watched the waves breaking. "Do you think that Mrs. Reddy made up the story about the zombie hitting the man in the head? Or do you think she heard it from someone else?"

"I don't know," Jessie said, tracing her finger through the sand. "It is always hard to tell where rumors start."

"One thing we do know," Henry said, "is that Mrs. Reddy certainly enjoys spreading rumors."

"I think she is just lonely and bored," Violet said. "I think she is sorry that she sold the amusement pier."

"I wonder what was she talking to Mr. Cooke about," Jessie said. "Do you think that Mr. Cooke and Mrs. Reddy could be working together to ruin Hanson's Amusement Pier?"

"Last time Benny and I saw Mr. Cooke and Mrs. Reddy together, they were fighting," Jessie said. "But today they were not. Mr. Cooke was smiling."

"I'm not sure if they are working together or not," Henry said. "But if Mr. Hanson cannot stop these rumors soon, his amusement pier will fail. No one will go there."

"We have to think of something to stop all these rumors," Violet said.

"Watch out!" Jessie cried.

A big wave came. It hit the castle and the walls fell away. Big chunks of sand slid into the ocean. Only the very top of the tower with the sea grass flag still stood.

"That was so cool," Benny said. "I love playing in the sand. Can we build another castle?"

"We can, but not right now," Jessie said. "I think we should go back to the house and get cleaned up. It is getting late."

The children splashed into the ocean and rinsed the sand from their arms and legs. They collected their things and walked back to the Hanson's beach house. Wendy waved to them from the porch.

"I was just going to come to look for you," she said. "How was the beach?"

"It was great!" Benny said. He told Wendy all about their sand castle and how the tide had come in and knocked it down.

"That does sound like fun," Wendy said. "Do you kids have any plans for tonight?"

"No," Jessie said. "We have not planned anything."

"I hate to ask this," Wendy said. "You have already done so much to help. But my father has lost two more employees today. There are so many rumors. People think that the amusement pier is unsafe. They think it is going to close soon. My father could really use your help tonight."

"Of course we'll help," Jessie said.

"We'll be glad to," Violet added.

The children showered and dressed. They rinsed their bathing suits and hung them to dry out on the line in the sun. Benny had a small collection of seashells that he had found. He set them in a pile by the steps.

Benny sat beside the shells. "Jessie, do you think I could buy a big bucket to put my shells in?" he asked.

"I think that is a good idea," Jessie said.

"We should get some shovels, too, Benny," Henry said. "We can build an even bigger castle with shovels."

"I would like to stop in the souvenir shop as well," Violet said. "I want to buy something to remember our trip."

"We should leave right away," Jessie said. "That way we will have time to go into the stores before we are needed at the amusement pier."

"I'll be right out," Violet said. Violet went back into the house. She wanted to get her money from her bedroom. She had just opened her drawer and was looking through her things when she heard Wendy and Will talking in the hallway.

"Did the kids leave yet?" Will asked in a quiet voice.

"Yes," Wendy said. "Did you get the zombie back in place in the haunted house?"

"Dad was working on it," Will said. "But there is a bolt missing. I don't know if the zombie will be working by tonight if we can't find that bolt."

"Where could it be?" Wendy asked. "Are you sure that you don't have it?"

"I don't have it, Wendy," Will said.

"Okay. I'm just checking," Wendy said. "Because we agreed that our plan was . . ."

Violet felt uncomfortable listening to a private conversation. She grabbed her money and closed the drawer very loudly.

Wendy and Will stopped talking. Wendy peeked around the corner and into Violet's room. "Violet!" she said. "I thought you had gone to the boardwalk."

"I forgot my money," Violet said. "I want to buy a souvenir in one of the shops. I am leaving now."

Violet joined Henry, Jessie, and Benny

outside, and the children headed down the boardwalk. On the way, Violet told her sister and brothers what she had overheard.

"What kind of plan do you think Wendy meant?" Jessie asked.

"I don't know," Violet said. "And why would Wendy think that Will had the missing bolt?"

"It could be that Will misplaced the bolt when he was putting the zombie back," Henry said. "Sometimes, when I am fixing things, I misplace a bolt or a screw. It can happen very easily."

"Look!" Benny cried. "Here is the store! Can we go in?"

At the Beach Stop Shop, Benny picked out a blue bucket and a large red shovel. Violet found a small jewelry box decorated from top to bottom with very tiny seashells.

Then the children paid for their purchases and left the store. They soon passed a woman in a white apron and a tall chef's hat. She stood outside Laura's Fudge Shop with a tray. "Would you like to try some of our fudge for free?" she asked the children.

"Free fudge! I would like some," Benny cried. He tried the chocolate peanut butter flavor. "It's so good!" he said.

"I'm glad you like it," the woman said. "We also have delicious saltwater taffy."

Benny shivered. He remembered when he accidentally got saltwater in his mouth when he was boogie boarding with Hunter. It did not taste good. "You put saltwater in your taffy?" he asked.

The woman laughed. "No. There is no saltwater in our saltwater taffy."

"Then why is it called that?" Benny asked.

"A very long time ago, a man had a taffy stand on the boardwalk in Atlantic City," the woman explained. "One night a big wave came and hit his stand. It ruined all his taffy. He was upset. He had nothing to sell the next day. When a customer asked for taffy, the man said that all he had to sell was saltwater taffy. He had to throw all the taffy away. The man worked hard and made more taffy. But he thought the name saltwater taffy was catchy. And he was right! We still call it saltwater taffy more than one hundred years later!"

The woman reached into her apron pocket. She pulled out some saltwater taffy. She gave one to each of the Aldens. "Try some," she said.

Benny took a bite of the soft candy. "This one tastes like peppermint!" he said. The soft and chewy candy seemed to melt in his mouth.

"Mine is butterscotch," Violet said. She laughed after she took a bite.

"Thank you very much," Jessie said, swallowing a chocolate-flavored taffy. "It is delicious. We will stop back later to buy some more! We don't have time right now."

"You kids are in a hurry?" the woman asked.

"Yes," Jessie said. "We are on our way to Hanson's Amusement Pier."

The woman looked concerned. "Be careful, kids," she said. "I've heard that it might not be safe at the pier."

"Someone is spreading false rumors," Jessie

said. "Please do not believe them. The pier is very safe."

The children thanked the woman and left.

"It was nice of that lady to give us free samples," Benny said.

"Yes, and smart, too," Violet said. "It makes us want to go back and buy more candy. And it has given me a very good idea for Hanson's Amusement Pier."

"Free candy?" Benny asked.

"No," Violet said. "Something even better. Something that will help stop all of the false rumors."

CHAPTER 9

Violet Has an Idea

The children found Mr. Hanson sitting in his shed at the back of the pier. There were tools all around him on his workbench, but he was not working.

"Hi, kids," Mr. Hanson said. "Thanks for coming. But I'm not sure that I will need your help tonight."

"Is something wrong?" asked Jessie.

Mr. Hanson pointed toward the door. "Did you see how few customers there are out there? Everyone thinks my pier is unsafe.

Even the local safety inspector heard the rumors. He stopped by today for a surprise inspection."

"Were there any problems?" Jessie asked.

"No, not at all," Mr. Hanson said. He showed Jessie the copy of the inspector's report. "The inspector congratulated me on my pier. He said it was very safe. I could post the report outside, but no one will see it. I do not know how to fight these false rumors."

"We have heard the rumors, too," Henry said "But Violet has come up with a wonderful idea."

Violet stood in front of the workbench. "Mr. Hanson," she said, "if we could only get people to come visit your pier, they would see how much fun it is and how it is safe. They would want to come back and visit many times."

Mr. Hanson held up his hand. "Thank you, Violet. I agree with you. But I cannot get people to come here. Did you see Bob Cooke's pier? There are long lines for all the rides. My rides are empty."

"But what if you had a special night where all the rides on Hanson's pier were free? I think many people would come for free rides. Then they would see how wonderful your pier is. The rumors would die because people would see the truth, that you have a safe and fun amusement pier."

Mr. Hanson sat up straight in his chair. He looked at Violet. "Violet," he said, "may I shake your hand?"

Violet's face was flushed. Mr. Hanson grabbed her hand and shook it up and down. There was a big smile on his face. "You are a genius!" he said. "I think it is a great plan. We should have the free night as soon as possible! I think we should do it tomorrow!"

The children looked at each other. "We would have to let everyone know first," Henry said.

"I'll put an ad in the paper," Mr. Hanson said, clapping his hands together.

"I can make flyers," Violet said. "We can put them up all around the boardwalk so that everyone will know about the special night."

"There is a T-shirt shop on the boardwalk," Jessie added. "We could have special shirts made that advertise the free night. We could wear them all day tomorrow."

Just then Will and Wendy walked into the shed. "Dad," Will said, "I found the bolt that you were looking for. I want to apologize. The bolt was in my . . ."

"Listen to this, Will!" Mr. Hanson said. "The Aldens have come up with a plan to save the pier." Mr. Hanson explained the plan to Will and Wendy.

"It sounds great!" Will said. "Wendy and I will help, of course."

There was no time to spare. Mr. Hanson headed straight to the *Oceanside Times* newspaper office to place a big ad for the next day's edition. Will and Henry went to the haunted house to put the bolt back on the zombie. Jessie, Violet, and Benny walked to the T-shirt shop and Wendy stayed to run the pier while everyone was gone.

The Oceanside Shirt Shop was a small store crowded with many racks of T-shirts.

"May I help you?" asked a young man behind the counter.

"Yes," Violet answered. "We would like to purchase some T-shirts, but can we make our own design to put on them?"

"Of course," the man answered.

Violet worked on the T-shirt design with the man while Jessie and Benny picked out a pile of plain green T-shirts in different sizes.

The man's name was Dennis. He was impressed with Violet's design. "You are a very

good artist," he said. "Is Hanson's pier really going to let people ride for free tomorrow?"

"Yes," Violet said.

"But is it safe? I have heard some bad rumors about Hanson's," Dennis said.

"They are false rumors that someone has been spreading," Violet explained. "The safety inspector checked out the whole pier today and he said it was very safe."

"That is good to hear," Dennis said. "I have a little boy. I will bring him over tomorrow to ride the rides. And I will tell my customers all about it, too."

Dennis finished pressing Violet's design onto the T-shirts and handed them to the children.

"Look at me!" Benny cried. Benny had put his small T-shirt on. "If I run up and down the boardwalk, everyone will know about the free night at Hanson's! I am a walking flyer!"

Jessie and Violet changed into their shirts as well. Then the children headed back toward the amusement pier. They noticed that people were staring at their shirts.

"Free rides!" The children heard a woman shout, and they turned. It was Mrs. Reddy. She was hurrying toward them.

"Hanson is giving out free rides?" she asked. "He must be crazy. He cannot make money if he gives the rides for free. He will be ruined." Mrs. Reddy looked toward the pier. "I know I could run it again," she said. "I do know a lot about running that pier. And my pier was always safe. I could be very helpful there."

"Hanson's pier is safe, Mrs. Reddy," Jessie said. "The safety inspector declared today that the pier is very safe. Someone has been spreading false rumors. The free rides are just for one night so that everyone can see how fun Hanson's pier is."

Violet turned toward the old woman. "I am sure that the pier was wonderful when you ran it, Mrs. Reddy," she said. "And I am sure that you must miss being in charge there. But it is still a very fun and very safe place."

"Would you like a T-shirt?" Benny asked. "It is free!"

Mrs. Reddy looked startled. "You are giving me a free T-shirt?"

"Sure," Benny said. "Why not?"

Mrs. Reddy took the T-shirt. "Thank you," she said. "I must admit, this is a very good idea. I never had T-shirts made when I owned the pier. I never thought of it! And maybe I will stop by tomorrow night to see how everything is going. If it gets very busy, maybe Carl will ask me to help."

When Jessie, Violet, and Benny got back to the pier, they went straight to the workshop. Mr. Hanson, Henry, Will, Wendy, and Hunter were sitting around the large wooden table. They were very impressed with the T-shirts. They each took one.

Mr. Hanson told them about the ad he had placed in the paper. "And Donna Mancini, the photographer, has been taking lots of pictures of the boardwalk. I am going use some of her pictures of the pier and put more ads in newspapers and magazines."

"What a wonderful idea," Violet said.

"My dad is donating pizza from his

shop," Hunter said. "The first one hundred customers tomorrow night will get a coupon for a free slice of pizza."

At the mention of the word pizza, there was a strange growling noise in the shed. "What was that?" Hunter asked.

"I'm sorry!" Benny's face turned very red. "But my stomach heard you say 'free pizza.'"

Everyone laughed.

"Why don't you go get something to eat? And then head back to the house and rest. Tomorrow will be a very busy day and we will need everyone's help."

The children stopped at Mack's and ordered take-out. They carried their dinners back to the Hansons' home and sat outside on the deck overlooking the ocean.

Jessie poured four glasses of cold milk. "Mr. Hanson has said that he will have to move back to Colorado if the amusement pier fails."

"That would be terrible!" Violet said. "Owning the amusement pier and living in this house on the beach was always Mr. Hanson's dream."

Henry took a bite of his cheesesteak. He looked thoughtful. "That is true, Violet. This is Mr. Hanson's dream. But I don't think that Wendy and Will had the same dream. I think they liked Colorado."

"Do you suspect them of trying to ruin the amusement pier?" Violet asked.

Henry took a long drink of milk. "I don't know," he said. "But remember that they both had red stains on their shoes, just like the red paint from the house of mirrors. And if the amusement pier fails, they would get to go back to Colorado to their old school and all their old friends."

"And remember that I accidently over-heard them talking in the hallway the other day." Violet sprinkled cheese on her pasta. "Wendy said that they had a 'plan.' I wonder what that meant."

Jessie had her notebook on the table and was looking through the clues she had written down. "And didn't Will say that he had the bolt to the zombie in his pocket? How did he get it?"

"He could have found it on the floor in the haunted house," Violet said.

Jessie tapped a pencil on her notebook. "What about Mrs. Reddy?"

"She spreads bad rumors," Benny said.

"That's right, Benny," Henry said. "Mrs. Reddy seems like she would be happy if the amusement pier failed. I think she is sorry that she sold it. She wants to run it again. She does not like being retired."

"But she did like the T-shirt we gave her. She said she would wear it." Benny said.

"Don't forget about Mr. Cooke," Violet said. "He also would like to run the amusement pier."

"That's true," Jessie said. "When he was arguing with Mrs. Reddy, he said that he wanted Mr. Hanson to fail. And someone with a black marker wrote on the walls of the house of mirrors. We found a marker with 'Captain Cooke's Amazing Amusement Pier' written on the side."

"But Mr. Cooke is right," Violet said. "There are many markers like that on the boardwalk. Anyone could have used it. But I agree that he acts suspicious sometimes. Remember the other day when we saw him on the boardwalk? His pants and shoes looked very wet. And it was not raining. He hurried away when he saw us looking at him."

"He might have been fixing a ride on his pier," Henry said. "He does have a log flume and a boat ride."

The children finished their meals and cleaned up the little table on the deck. Violet leaned on the rail. She stared out at the moonlight glinting off of the ocean. She wished she could take a photograph of the view and save it. She thought of Mrs. Mancini, the photographer who took so many pictures of Oceanside.

Suddenly, Violet stood up straight. She turned to her sister and brothers. "I have an idea," she said. "I think I know how we might catch the people who are trying to ruin the pier."

CHAPTER 10

An Accidental Confession

Early the next morning, the children started their day at Dottie's Pancake House. They wore the T-shirts that Violet had designed. Everyone in the small restaurant asked them about the free rides. The people seemed excited and made plans to visit Hanson's Amusement Pier.

Dottie, the woman who owned the restaurant, stopped at the children's table. "How is everything?" she asked.

Benny tried to answer, but his mouth was stuffed with pancakes.

Jessie was cutting up her French toast. She laughed. "I think you can see that our brother loves your pancakes. Everything here is wonderful."

Dottie smiled. "Thank you. I noticed your T-shirts," she said. "Everyone is talking about them. Are the rides really free tonight?"

"Yes, they are," Jessie answered.

Dottie smiled. "Maybe I will stop by and check it out tonight."

After breakfast the children visited a copy store. The night before, Violet had designed the flyer that would advertise the free night. It looked a lot like the design on the T-shirts. The man made the copies for the children right away.

Next to the copy store was the photographer's shop. Violet gazed in the window at all the beautiful photographs. Ms. Mancini had many colorful pictures of sunsets over the bay, shore birds, and happy families posing on the beach. A sign on the door said, "Out taking photographs. Be back soon!"

As the children walked farther down the

street, they saw a shop that rented bicycles. Bikes in every size lined the sidewalk.

"Look!" Violet cried. "They even rent surreys!"

"What is a surrey?" Benny asked.

Violet walked up to the surrey and showed Benny. The surrey had four wheels and four sets of pedals. It had two seats in front and two in the back. There was a steering wheel, just like a car, and there was a yellow and blue striped cloth roof over the top.

A woman in a blue apron walked up to the children. "Would you like to rent the surrey?" she asked. "They are lots of fun."

The children agreed. They paid the woman and climbed in. Henry and Jessie sat up front. Violet and Benny were in the back. With all four children pedaling, the surrey could go quite fast. They took turns driving. Even Benny had a turn! As they rode back down the boardwalk, they made many stops and posted the flyers in stores and on announcement boards.

Henry looked at his watch. "It is almost

ten o'clock," he said. "We should return the surrey now to the rental store."

The children pedaled back the way they had come. "Look," Benny said. "Isn't that Mr. Cooke?"

"It is," Jessie said. "What is he carrying?"

"I don't know," Henry said. "It looks like big poster boards. Maybe he is making signs for his pier, too."

After the children returned the surrey, they got right to work. Henry and Benny took half of the remaining flyers and Jessie and Violet took the other half.

"Benny and I will give these out on the beach," Henry said.

"And we will hand them out on the boardwalk," Jessie said.

But before the children could start, they

saw Mr. Hanson hurrying toward them. He had a worried look on his face.

"What's wrong?" the children asked.

Mr. Hanson wrung his hands together. "I don't know exactly. I just got a call from Ms. Mancini, the photographer, that she saw something wrong at the pier. We don't open for a few more hours. I hope it is something I can fix."

Everyone hurried toward the pier. They saw the problem right away.

"Oh no!" Violet said. "Who could have done such a thing?"

The top six cars on the giant Ferris wheel each had a very large letter pasted to its side. All together, the cars spelled out the word "UNSAFE." It was so big, everyone on the boardwalk could see what it said. Ms. Mancini was standing nearby taking photographs.

They all hurried to the Ferris wheel. Mr. Hanson pulled his keys from his pocket. He turned the Ferris wheel on so that the cars at the top moved to the bottom. Ms. Mancini and the children helped him remove the letters. It was not hard. The letters had been printed on white poster board and taped to the sides of the car.

"Who else has keys to the Ferris wheel?" Henry asked.

Mr. Hanson was ripping the cardboard letters into pieces. "Only Wendy, Will, and I have keys," he said. "And I suppose Mrs. Reddy might. She was supposed to turn over all the keys to me when I bought the pier. But I suppose that it is possible that she kept some."

"What about Mr. Cooke?" asked Jessie.

Mr. Hanson shook his head. "Mr. Cooke would not have any keys to my pier."

"Is there any other way to get the letters up on those cars?" Henry asked.

Mr. Hanson looked up at the Ferris wheel. "I suppose you could climb up," he said. "It's not too hard. But most people would be afraid to do such a thing."

"I took a lot of pictures of your pier over the last week," Ms. Mancini said. "I will develop them and leave them in your workshop. I don't know if they will help. But maybe they will show something that will help you to figure out who is doing these things. I will drop them off around four o'clock."

The Alden children looked at one another and smiled. This would help their plan.

Mr. Hanson thanked Ms. Mancini. He asked the Aldens if they could help him to look through the pictures. Everyone agreed to meet in the workshop at about five o'clock. Henry and Benny then headed toward the beach to distribute their flyers.

Jessie and Violet walked up and down the boardwalk to hand out their flyers. Just as they had hoped, they saw Mrs. Reddy. She was wearing the T-shirt that they had given her yesterday.

"Hello!" Mrs. Reddy waved to Jessie and Violet. "I am wearing my T-shirt," she said. "How does it look?"

"It looks very nice on you," Violet said. "Green is a good shade for you. It matches your eyes."

Mrs. Reddy smiled. "Thank you, Violet.

You are very sweet. Do you think anyone will come to Hanson's pier tonight?"

"Yes," Jessie said. "Many people will come."

"But what about that sign on the Ferris wheel?" Mrs. Reddy asked.

"We saw it," Jessie replied. "But Mr. Hanson has taken it down. And we hope to figure out who put it there. A photographer has been taking pictures of the pier. She is dropping them off in the work shed at four o'clock. We will look through them later for clues."

Mrs. Reddy put her hand up to her mouth. "Oh my," she said. "I wonder what those pictures will show. I better go. But I will stop by the pier later." Mrs. Reddy hurried away.

When Jessie and Violet got to Captain Cooke's amusement pier, they stood outside handing out the flyers until Mr. Cooke noticed and came rushing toward them.

"Get out of here with those flyers!" he said.

"You are wasting your time anyway. Hanson's pier is not safe and it will close before the summer is over."

"It is safe," Violet insisted.

"Didn't you see that sign on the Ferris wheel?" Mr. Cooke said.

"Yes," Violet answered. "We saw it. But it is nothing more than a mean trick. It does not mean that the pier is unsafe."

"Then why would someone go to all the trouble to put that sign up?" Mr. Cooke asked.

"We don't know," Jessie answered. "But we may have a clue."

Mr. Cooke's eyebrows went up. "Really? What kind of clue?"

Jessie explained about Ms. Mancini's photographs. "She has been taking photographs all over the boardwalk. She has many of Hanson's pier. No one really noticed that she was there. We are going to the work shed at five o'clock to look through the photographs. They might show who has been trying to ruin Mr. Hanson."

Mr. Cooke's face turned red. "Those photographs probably won't show a thing!"

he said. "What time did you say that Mrs. Mancini is dropping off the photos?"

"At four o'clock in the work shed," Violet answered.

Mr. Cooke turned away. "I have a busy night ahead of me," he said. "I have to get back to work. And keep those flyers away from my pier!"

After Henry and Benny were finished on the beach, they met Jessie and Violet at a lemonade stand on the boardwalk.

The children bought lemonades and walked out over the ocean.

"I sure hope everything works out tonight," Benny said. "Some people on the beach said that they saw the 'unsafe' sign on the Ferris wheel."

"I think people will be curious about the free rides," Henry said. "They will come and see how safe the amusements are. I just hope that there are no more pranks tonight. I hope our plan works."

Jessie took a long sip from her cool drink. "Violet and I saw Mrs. Reddy and Mr. Cooke on the boardwalk this morning," she said. "We told them that Mrs. Mancini had some photographs that might contain clues as to who has been trying to ruin Mr. Hanson's pier."

Violet nodded. "We told them that the photographs would be dropped off at the work shed at four o'clock."

"Mrs. Reddy loves to spread news on the boardwalk. I am sure she will tell many people," Jessie said.

"Now I get it!" Benny said. "The person who has been playing all the mean tricks will want to steal the photos in case he or she is in them!"

"Exactly!" Jessie said.

The children agreed that they would arrive early at the work shed to see who might show up after Mrs. Mancini dropped off the photos. In the meantime, they relaxed on the beach. They talked about all the things they had seen and all the clues they had gathered. Jessie wrote everything down in her notebook.

When the Aldens returned to Hanson's pier later in the afternoon, they went straight to the work shed as planned. They were surprised to find Wendy and Will sitting with their father on a bench. He had his arms around them.

"We're sorry," Jessie said. "We did not mean to intrude. We will come back later. We thought we would come a little early."

"Please stay," Mr. Hanson said. "Wendy, Will, and I were just having a long talk. I now realize that we should have talked a long time ago. I didn't take their feelings into account when we moved to Oceanside."

"Dad, it's okay," Wendy said. "Everything is fine now."

"Yes," Will said. "We weren't fair to you either, Dad. In the beginning, we did not give Oceanside a chance. We thought that if you had a lot of problems with the pier, you would not like it here. We wanted you to hate running the amusement pier. We thought you would let us move back to Colorado."

"You were the ones who splashed the red

paint in the house of mirrors," Jessie said. "You were careful, but some of the paint splattered onto your shoes."

Wendy and Will looked down at their feet. "Yes," Will said. "You're right, Jessie. A house of mirrors is not fun if you can see where you are going. We're very sorry, Dad."

"We want to apologize to Benny, too," Wendy said.

Mr. Hanson looked confused. "Benny? What did you do to Benny?"

Wendy rubbed the top of Benny's head, but she was too embarrassed to speak.

"Will and Wendy took the zombie from the haunted house," Henry explained. "I am sure that they did not know that Benny would be there. The zombie is very heavy, and Will must have accidentally hit Benny in the face when he was moving it. It was very dark."

Mr. Hanson turned to Henry. "You knew that Will took the zombie?"

"Not right away," Henry said. "We could not accuse him. But there were clues. Today on the beach, we put all the clues together."

"I was on top of the Big Slide," Violet explained. "I saw someone going down the steps toward the beach carrying the zombie."

"And at the same time," Jessie added, "the haunted house ride was turned on. So it had to be two people working together."

"And they had to have had a key to turn the ride on," Henry said.

"Will and Wendy had a spare key," Jessie said. "We heard Wendy say so the next day."

"It was very dark in the haunted house that night. I'm sorry, Benny," Will said. "It was an accident. Wendy turned on the ride so that the lights would come on. She knew that your brother and sisters would come and help you."

Mr. Hanson listened in amazement. "You should have stayed and helped Benny yourselves!" he said. "You should not have left him there."

"We know," Wendy said. "We're so sorry."

"We feel terrible about what we have done," Will said. "But now we know that Oceanside is a wonderful place. We understand why you wanted to move here. And we have met some very nice friends."

Just then Ms. Mancini stepped inside the shed. She handed a stack of photographs to Mr. Hanson. "I took a quick look through the photos. They don't really show anything that would help you catch the person who has been playing the tricks," she said. "I'm sorry. But there are some nice shots that we can use for advertisements."

Mr. Hanson glanced through the photos. He held up the one of the Ferris wheel with the word *unsafe* on the cars. "Did you do this, too?" he asked Wendy and Will.

Suddenly, the doorknob of the small work shed began to rattle. Everyone grew quiet. The door slowly creaked open. A head peered around the side of the door.

"Bob!" Mr. Hanson cried. "What are you doing here?"

Mr. Cooke looked startled to see the room so full of people. He looked down at his watch. "It is not five o'clock yet. I . . . I just came to see if . . . I mean, to say good luck tonight."

Jessie pointed to the stack of photographs in Mr. Hanson's hands. "Are you sure you did not come for the photographs, Mr. Cooke?" she asked.

"But how did Bob know we had the photographs?" Mr. Hanson asked. "I don't understand."

"Those kids told me," Mr. Cooke said. "So you have looked through the photographs already?" he asked.

"Yes, we have," Mr. Hanson answered.

Mr. Cooke shoved his hands deep into his pockets. "Then you know that I am the one who put the word *unsafe* on the Ferris wheel. But it was just a joke, Carl."

"Actually, Bob," Mr. Hanson said, "the photographs don't show you at all."

"What?!" Mr. Cooke turned toward the Aldens. "Those kids told me that the photos had clues in them."

"We did not," Violet responded. "We said that we hoped that there were clues in them. But you have just admitted that you put the word *unsafe* on the Ferris wheel."

"But how did you get up there?" Benny asked. "It is so high!"

"I fix rides all the time. I know how to go up and down them. I have my own Ferris wheel on my pier, remember?" Mr. Cooke turned toward Mr. Hanson. "And my Ferris wheel has always been better than yours! I was just trying to protect the public from this unsafe pier."

"You were not protecting the public when you put the zombie in the ocean," Henry said.

Mr. Cooke looked startled.

"It was you," Jessie said. "We saw you later walking down the boardwalk and your pants and shoes were quite wet. You did not seem to care that a swimmer banged his ankle against the zombie in the water."

"You wanted Mr. Hanson to be blamed for it," Violet said.

"And Mr. Cooke wrote with black marker in the house of mirrors," Benny added.

Mr. Hanson looked upset. "Did you really do all these things, Bob?" he asked.

Mr. Cooke looked around the room.

Everyone was staring at him. "I . . . I . . . All right, I admit it! I did those things. But so what? It is just a little friendly competition."

"There is nothing friendly about it," Mr. Hanson said. "I want you to leave my amusement pier right now. And don't ever set foot here again or I will call the police. You are lucky I am not calling the police right now!"

Mr. Cooke's face turned very red. Then he hurried out of the shed.

A few moments later, there was knock on the door. "Carl? Are you in there?"

Mr. Hanson opened the door. "Mrs. Reddy! Come in. What are you doing here?"

Mrs. Reddy cleared her throat. "I um . . . I want to apologize."

"More apologies!" Mr. Hanson exclaimed. "What could you have done, Mrs. Reddy?"

"Mrs. Reddy wanted your pier to fail also," Jessie said. "She misses being the owner and running the pier. She thinks that she made a mistake to retire. She would like to run the pier again."

Mrs. Reddy nodded. "Jessie is right. So many things were going wrong here, I thought that you would ruin the pier. And I was bored at home with not much to do. I love this pier. I want to keep it great. It is the best pier on the boardwalk."

Mr. Hanson nodded. "I know how you feel. And I sure could use your help," he said. "You have so much experience. Would you be willing to help out here?"

Mrs. Reddy smiled. "Really? You would let me help? I would love to!"

There was another knock at the door.

Mr. Hanson scratched his head. "Now what?" he said.

It was Madison, one of the pier workers. "Mr. Hanson!" she cried. "We need your help out here!"

"What is the problem?" Mr. Hanson asked.

Madison's face was flushed. "There are so many customers, we need help running the rides! I think the whole town of Oceanside has come to your pier tonight!"

"How wonderful!" Violet said.

Everyone rushed out to help run the pier. Jessie sold tickets. Henry and Benny ran the haunted house ride. Violet helped children on the Big Slide. Mrs. Reddy went from ride to ride, helping wherever she was needed, and smiling happily at all the customers. She told everyone what a safe and wonderful pier Carl Hanson was running. Wendy ran the motorcycle ride and Will took care of the Ferris wheel.

When the pier finally closed, all of the customers went away talking about how much fun they had had.

"We will be back!" many people called as they walked away. "Thank you so much for a great night."

Mr. Hanson, Will, Wendy, Mrs. Reddy, and the Aldens sat at a picnic table at the end of the pier overlooking the ocean. They were very tired.

"The free ride night was a big success," Jessie said. "Now everyone knows that Hanson's is a terrific and safe amusement pier."

"Yes." Mr. Hanson smiled. "Thanks to you children."

Suddenly, there was a loud growling sound. Mrs. Reddy looked startled. She put her hand over her heart. "What was that?" she asked.

Everyone turned to look at Benny. Benny held his stomach. "I can't help it!" he said. "My stomach always does that when I am hungry."

"And Benny is always hungry," Henry explained.

"Then I am just in time!" Hunter walked up to the picnic table. His arms were full of boxes of pizza from Mack's.

"Oh boy!" Benny cried. "Mack's has the best pizza in the world. It smells so good!"

"Congratulations, Mr. Hanson," Hunter said. "Everyone on the boardwalk has been talking about your amusement pier. The free ride night must have been a great success."

"It was," Mr. Hanson said. "And it is not over yet."

Benny swallowed a big mouthful of pepperoni pizza. "It's not over yet?" He looked around. "But all the customers are gone. I thought the pier was closed."

Mr. Hanson smiled. "The pier is closed, but we are still here. And now that the crowds are gone, I think you children should try all the rides."

Benny jumped up from the table. "Really? Can I ride the motorcycles? And the roller coaster? And the Ferris wheel, too?"

"Of course you can," Will said. "And you can ride them as many times as you like."

"I'm going to ride everything!" Benny said. Then he paused. "Except maybe not the haunted house. The zombies still scare me a little bit. I know they are not real but . . ."

Just then another long, loud growl came from Benny's stomach.

Mrs. Reddy laughed. "Benny, I think the zombies should be afraid of your stomach! It sounds much scarier than they do."

"You're right, Mrs. Reddy!" Benny grabbed another piece of pizza and headed toward the haunted house. "Okay, zombies, here I come," he called. "I am not afraid of you!"

Everyone laughed. Henry, Jessie, Violet, Benny, Will, Wendy, Hunter, Mr. Hanson, and even Mrs. Reddy spent a fun night riding on all the rides, playing games, and eating the pizza that Hunter had brought.

"Mr. Hanson," Benny said at the end of the night, holding his very full stomach, "I hope that you own this amusement pier forever and ever!"

"We all do," Violet said.

Mr. Hanson smiled. He put one arm around Will and one around Wendy. He gazed up at the big Ferris wheel. "This has always been my dream," he said. "And now, because of all of you, my dream has come true! Thank you!"